Sam
the Big, Bad Cat

Written by Sheila Bird
Illustrated by Trish Phillips

Collins

Tom had a big, bad cat called Sam. One day Sam didn't feel well.

2

Tom said, "I'll take you
to the vet."

Sam didn't want to go
to the vet.

He ran away and hid
under his bed.
Tom found him.

Sam hid under the table.

Tom found him.

Sam hid in the cupboard.

Tom found him.

Sam hid in the shower.

Tom found him.
Tom got very wet.

Tom said, "I don't feel well
at all. I'm going to bed."

Sam was feeling much
better.

A storyboard

 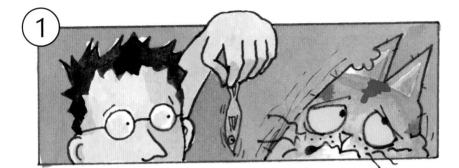 

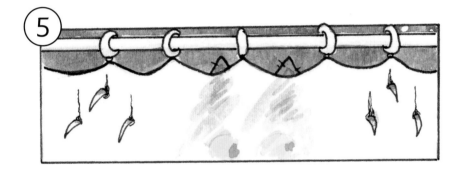

Ideas for reading

Written by Alison Tyldesley MA PGCE
Education, Childhood and Inclusion Lecturer

Learning objectives: Pointing while reading; using a variety of cues to work out unfamiliar words; blending and reading CVC words; reading initial and final phonemes; identifying and discussing characters and their actions; exploring themes and characters through role-play.

Curriculum links: Citizenship: animals and us

High frequency words: a, big, cat, said, I, to, the, in

Interest words: vet, found, under, cupboard, shower, better

Word count: 86

Getting started

- Discuss the front cover with the children and introduce the character of Sam. Read the title – what tells you Sam is a bad cat on the front cover?

- Walk through the book and discuss the pictures up to p11. Why is Sam trying to hide? How does Tom feel on p11?

- Discuss the new words in the story and ask children to point to them, e.g. *found, under*. Demonstrate how to read following print with eyes but pointing at difficult words.

- Ask the children to find the CVC words on p2 (*Tom, had, big, bad, cat, Sam, well*). Ask them to read out each word (sound them out). Point out that 'll' makes one sound.

Reading and responding

- Read the first two pages together, then ask the children to read independently up to p11. Praise reading and pointing at difficult words. Prompt the children to use a variety of cues to read unfamiliar words.

- At this point, ask the children to predict what happens at the end of the story. Do they think Tom will take Sam to the vet? Why not? Then they can read on to p13 to find out if they were right.